Keep asking BIG
questions ! Trust that
God knows the way!

[signature]

How Can I Choose?

Written by
Robin W. Hurst

Illustrated by
Award-Winning Artist,
Rosemarie Gillen

Avid Christian Books
Lakewood, California

How Can I Choose?

Avid Christian Books

http://www.avidchristianbooks.com

ISBN-13: 978-1-61286-231-6

Printed in the United States

Dedication

I dedicate this book in loving memory of my courageous and precious niece, Samantha Laux, who continues to stir my heart.

I thank God for his unfailing love and never ending grace.

I am richly blessed by my loving husband, Ken, who believes in me, always.

I give special thanks to...

Mom, Jane Wingerd, who generously supported me to "follow through on a new start" and a dream that I could have believed was not enough.

Dad, Robert Wingerd, (aka "Dr. Bob" to so many), who always modeled love, kindness, patience, gentleness, peace, self-control, goodness, faithfulness, joy, and laughter.

My sister, Gail Laux, and her daughter, Sarah, who helped me see the pages through the eyes of children.

My brother, Dave Wingerd, who can lift my spirit just by entering the room. I watch him do this for our parents as well and this, is a very special gift.

I am also grateful for my dear friends who have filled my spirit with encouragement along my path. Without your cheers from the balcony, I may not have been able to move faithfully forward.

Meet Gracie
and her faithful dog, ENUF.

How can I choose
the less traveled path
when others I know
have more than I have?

Trust me, Gracie

Your answer is "trust me"?
Is that all you've got?
Just love and believe
that my fear is for naught?

But when I look left and then to the right, others have confidence for this I must fight!

I do want to trust you.
I know you're enough.
My heart says you're with me,
but believing is tough.

You ask me to pause,
so, I ask for your help.
Please show me how greater
means less of myself.

11

Finish Line

But how can I pause
when the world is so fast?
Going too slow
just might make me last.

12

I give you my questions.
my worries, my doubts
and trust that you've got them
all figured out.

13

I'd thought that my questions
for you were not heard,
but you always listen
and you give me your Word.

that my life is rich,
my heart can expand
when I seek and I reach
and you give me your hand!

17

I feel like shouting
from mountain to stream
that you are here with me
and all in between!

May the world soon see that
the less traveled path
is the one that gives back
as soon as we ask.

As peace fills my body,
my heart and my mind,
your love provides strength
I hope others will find!

"My Grace is Enough..."
2 Cor. 12:9a (BET)

Amen

Questions about Gracie's journey:

1. Who is Gracie in conversation with on her journey?
2. What does God want us to have more than toys and stuff? Why?
3. What does winning really mean? Does it mean finishing first?
4. How can you give God your questions, worries and doubts?
5. What does the rainbow represent?
6. What are some of the choices God wants us to make every day?
7. Where can we find God?
8. Who does Gracie want to tell about what she has discovered?
9. Who is with Gracie on every page?
10. How is ENUF like God?
11. Why is God enough?

Further Insight to the Story Using God's Word
The Holy Bible

As you and your child, grandchild, niece, nephew, or loved one of any relationship read this book together, it is my hope and prayer that you will discover a new or deeper relationship with God. God is always ready and waiting for us to call out to Him. He is hopeful that we will listen for and be guided by His answers. I know that God loves you and that He has a very special plan for you.

*"For I know the plans I have for you, declares the Lord,
plans to prosper you and not to harm you,
plans to give you hope and a future. Then you will call
on me and come and pray to
me, and I will listen to you. You will seek me and find
me when you seek me with all your heart."
Jeremiah 29:11-13*

I hope you enjoy your own discovery of God's word as it relates to Gracie's encounters with Him. As you can see, Gracie's loyal companion, Enuf, never leaves her side. In many ways, Enuf represents God - always there, always faithful and always enough.

Pages 5 & 6 – Themes: Contentment / Comparison

How Can I choose the less traveled path, when others I know have more than I have? Not sure I'm ready to trade all my stuff for whatever you give that you say is enough.

Author Notes: Gracie is asking God how can she possibly take the path with less stuff, fewer toys, and all the stuff other kids seem to have. God is assuring her that joy, peace, and delight are not found through "stuff" but through a relationship with Him.

God does not intend for us to give up everything (our toys and stuff). Paul said in the Bible, (3 John 1:2 Amplified Bible), "Beloved, I pray that you may prosper in every way…" God wants us to prosper in all ways without fear. He simply wants our love for HIM to come FIRST in our hearts.

Matthew 6:21
For where your treasure is, there your heart will be also.

Colossians 3:2
Set your minds on things above, not on earthly things.

Proverbs 37:4
Delight yourself in the Lord and he will give you all the desires of your heart.

PAGES 7, 8 & 9 — Themes: Fear, Courage, Trust, God's Protection

Your answer is "trust me"? Is that all you've got? Just love and believe that my fear is for naught? Looking to left and then to the right, others have confidence for this I must fight!
Really? Lay it down, this fear that I feel? I'll feel so exposed, have no proper shield!

Author Notes: Gracie battles her fear and finds it difficult to simply trust God and to believe that he is with her every step of the way and that he provides all the armor she needs.

God's Word:
Genesis 15:1
Do not be afraid, I am your shield, your great reward.

2 Timothy 1:7 (KJV)
For God has not given us a spirit of fear, but of power and of love and of a sound mind.

Galations 5:22-23 (NLT)
But the holy Spirit produces this kind of fruit in our lives: love, joy, peace, patience, kindness, goodness, faithfulness, genteness, and self-control.

Psalm 138:3 (NIRV)
When I called out to you, you answered me. You made me strong and brave.

24

Page 10 – Themes: Belief, Trust, God's Love and Grace is Enough

I do want trust you. I know you're enough. My heart says you're with me, but believing is tough.

Author Notes: *Gracie is beginning to understand God's message but still struggles to accept it fully.*

God's Word:
Psalm 28:7 (NIV)

The LORD is my strength and my shield; my heart trusts in him, and he helps me. My heart leaps for joy, and with my song I praise him.

Phillipians 4:13 (NLT)

For I can do all things through Christ, who gives me strength.

2 Corinthians 12:9

My grace is sufficient for you, for my power is made perfect in your weakness.

Pages 11 & 12 – Themes: Slowing Down, Listening, God's Greatness

You ask me to pause, so I ask for your help. Please show me how greater means less of myself.
How can I pause when the world is so fast? Going too slow just might make me last!

Author Notes: *Gracie wants to slow down to listen to God, but needs his help to change her desire (will) to keep up with what others are doing in this fast, busy world.*

God's Word:
Jeremiah 6:16

Stand at the crossroads and look; ask for the ancient path, ask where the good way is; and walk in it, and you will find rest (peace) for your soul.

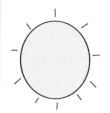

John 3:30
He (Jesus) must become greater; I must become less.

Psalm 130:5
I wait for the Lord, my whole being waits and in his word I put my hope.

Romans 12:2
Do not conform to the pattern of this world, but be transformed by the renewing of your mind.

Matthew 20:16
So the first will be last and the last will be first.

Page 13 –Themes: Surrender, God is Trustworthy and BIG!

I give you my questions, my worries, my doubts and trust that you've got them all figured out.

Author Notes: Gracie is beginning to understand how great God is and how trusting him can bring tremendous peace and confidence to rest in him.

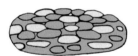

God's Word:
Psalm 46:10
Be still and know that I am God.

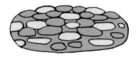

Phillipians 4:6-7
Do not be anxious about anything, but in every situation, by prayer and petition, with thanksgiving, present your requests to God. 7 And the peace of God, which transcends all understanding, will guard your hearts and your minds in Christ Jesus.

Pages 14 & 15 – Themes: God's Guidance, Our Free Will

I'd thought that my questions to you were not heard, but you always listen and you give me Your Word. You give me grace, love and peace too. I see how my choices can lead me to you.

Author Notes: *Gracie is beginning to pause and spend time with God. As she does she realizes God can lead her to make the right choices. Gracie knows that it can be hard to make the right choices, but she is learning that "right choices" bring great joy and freedom to her heart!*

God's Word:
Matthew 7:7

Ask and you shall receive, seek and you shall find, knock and the door will be opened unto you.

2 Samuel 7:28

O sovereign Lord you are God, your words are trustworthy.

Jeremiah 29:12-13

Then you will call on me and come and pray to me, and I will listen to you. You will seek me and find me when you seek me with all your heart.

Pages 16 & 17 — Themes: Fullness of God's Love
Amazing!
I see for the very first time. Letting go of my stuff helps me to find…
That my life is rich, my heart can expand when I seek and I reach and you give me your hand!

Author Notes: *Gracie is amazed to learn that when she gives away some of her toys and fears that God replaces those with something even better. Gracie's heart is so full.*

God's Word:
Psalms 16:11

You make known to me the path of life: you will fill me with joy in your presence.

Psalm 16:5

LORD, you alone are my portion and my cup; you make my lot secure.

Matthew 6:33

But seek first his kingdom and his righteousness, and all these things will be given to you as well.

Acts 17:27

God did this so that they would seek him and perhaps reach out for him and find him though he is not far away from any of us.

Pages 18 & 19 – Themes: God's Joy and Love

I feel like shouting from mountain to stream that you are here with me and all in between! May the world soon see the less traveled path is the one that gives back as soon as we ask.

Author Notes: *Gracie is so consumed with joy and excitement since she discovered God's never-ending love that she cannot wait to share what she has learned with others!*

God's Word:

2 Corinthians 3:17 (LEB)

Now the Lord is the Spirit, and where the Spirit of the Lord is, there is freedom.

John 3:16 (NLV)

For God so loved the world, He gave His one and only Son. Whoever puts his trust in God's Son will not be lost but will have life that lasts forever.

Isaiah 55:12

You will go out in joy and be led forth in peace; the mountains and hills will burst into song before you, and all the trees of the field will clap their hands.

Psalm 115:1

Not to us Lord, not to us, but to your name be the glory, because of your love and faithfulness.

Page 20 – Themes: God's Peace, Love and Hope

As peace fills my body, my heart and my mind your love provides strength I hope others will find!

Author Notes: Gracie, her loyal dog, Enuf, and her friends come together to share the joy. As they spend time with God and one another, they become excited to invite others to join them!

God's Word:

Romans 15:13

May the God of hope fill you with all joy and peace as you trust in him, so that you may overflow with hope by the power of the Holy Spirit.

John 14:27

Peace I leave with you, my peace I give to you; not as the world gives do I give to you.

1 Corinthians 13:4 & 8

Love is patient, love is kind. Love never fails.

Phillipians 4:7

The peace of God which transcends all understanding will guard your hearts and your minds in Christ Jesus.

God fills our hearts with HIS love, joy, and peace when we ask (invite) Him to do so. Receiving these gifts helps us to be more willing and excited to help others, share our "toys and stuff" and love one another. When we do, God can turn our fear into courage our doubt into trust. We can become content with less and confident that God will provide all we need – which is enough.

I hope you will read this little book many times over. My heart is full just knowing that it is in your hands right now.

Trusting in Him,
Robin

All scriptures are quoted from New International Version (NIV) of The Holy Bible, unless otherwise noted.

Robin, her husband, Ken and their dog, Lollie reside in Richmond, Virginia, still seeking answers but trusting that God knows the way.

Photograph of Robin Hurst and her dog Lollie by Nicki Metcalf Photography.

To schedule a book reading by the author, order a copy of the book or hire Robin to speak to a group, please visit

www.YourPathMatters.com
Or follow her on Facebook
at Your Path Matters™

Robin's unique and artistic "Your Path Matters® Jewelry" is also available to view on the website.

CPSIA information can be obtained
at www.ICGtesting.com
Printed in the USA
BVXC01n1836290914
368286BV00001B/1